Contents

Let's Draw!

Welcome to the world of drawing! In this book you'll learn how to draw all sorts of sea creatures in four easy steps. All you need is a pencil and paper, and some crayons, colored pencils, or markers for coloring in.

LET'S DRAW STEP BY STEP

Let's Draw SEA CREATURES

KASIA DUDZIUK

WINDMILL BOOKS

Published in 2020 by Windmill Books,
an Imprint of Rosen Publishing
29 East 21st Street, New York, NY 10010

Cataloging-in-Publication Data

Names: Dudziuk, Kasia.
Title: Let's draw sea creatures / Kasia Dudziuk.
Description: New York : Windmill Books, 2020. | Series: Let's draw step by step | Includes glossary and index.
Identifiers: ISBN 9781538391440 (pbk.) | ISBN 9781538391464 (library bound) | ISBN 9781538391457 (6 pack)
Subjects: LCSH: Marine animals in art--Juvenile literature. | Drawing--Technique--Juvenile literature.
Classification: LCC NC781.D839 2019 | DDC 743.6--dc23

Manufactured in the United States of America

CPSIA Compliance Information: Batch BS19WM: For Further Information contact Rosen Publishing, New York, New York at 1-800-237-9932

Lobster

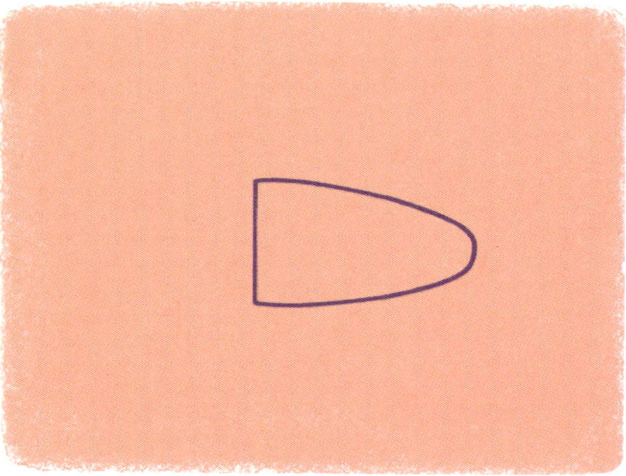

1 First, draw this shape for the head and body.

2 Add front legs and a tail.

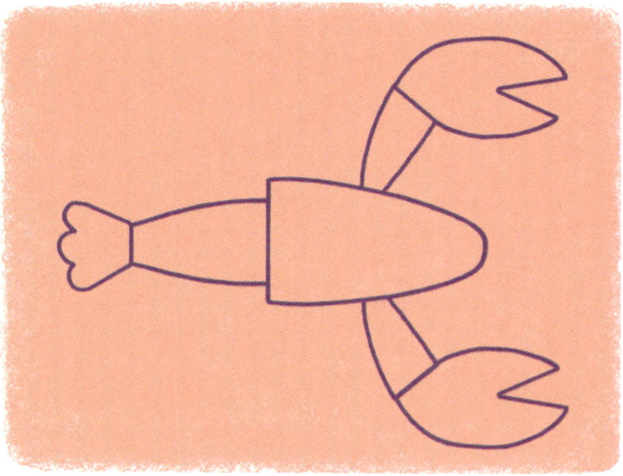

3 Draw the pincer claws and finish the tail.

4 Add the eyes, legs, and feelers. Color it bright red.

Seagull

1 Start by drawing this shape for the head.

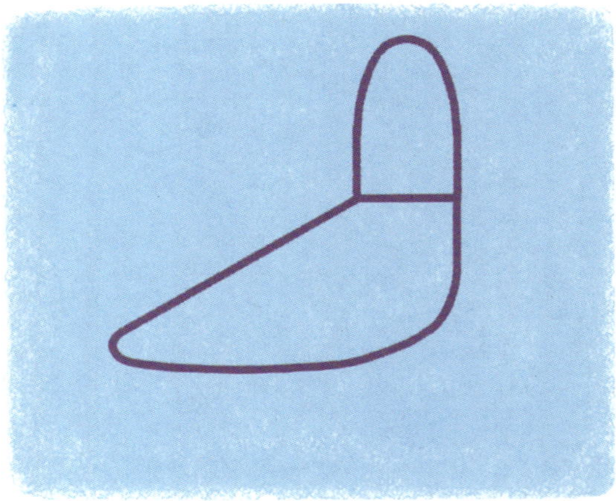

2 Now draw the body.

3 Add two legs.

4 Add an eye, wing, and yellow beak. Give the seagull orange legs.

Seagulls eat fish and crabs they catch on the seashore.

Sea Lion

1 Draw this shape for the body.
Leave a gap at the bottom.

2 Now add the flippers.

3 Draw a long body.

4 Draw the face and tail.
Color the sea lion in shades of brown.

Oyster

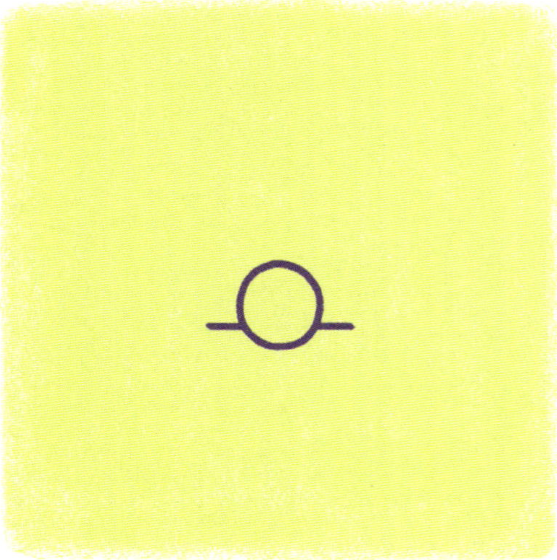

1 First draw the round pearl and a line for the hinge of the shell.

2 Draw the top and bottom of the shell with wavy edges.

3 Add a curved line around the edges to finish the oyster.

4 Draw the ridges of the shell and color it in pale shades with a white pearl.

Starfish

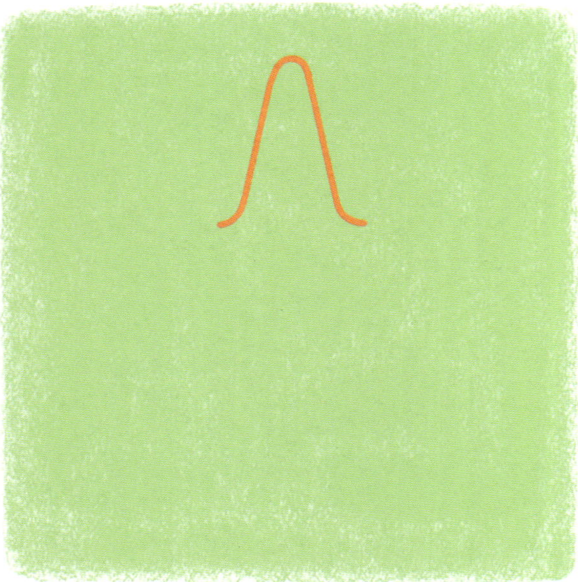

1 Start with the arm at the top of the starfish.

2 Add the two side arms.

3 Now add the two arms at the bottom.

4 Give it a happy face. Color it in a lovely shade of orange.

Starfish come in lots of different shapes and sizes!

Most starfish have five arms that are the same length.

Clown Fish

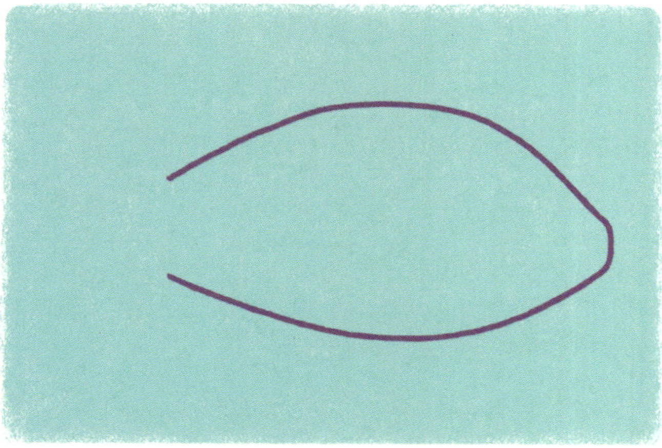

1 Draw this shape for the body, leaving a gap for the tail.

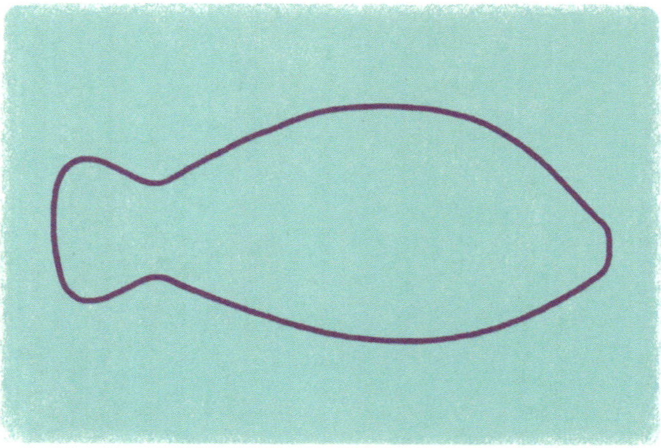

2 Now add the tail fin.

3 Draw two fins on the top, one on the bottom, and one on the side.

4 Draw a face and color orange and white stripes on the fish. Make the tips of the fins black.

Clown fish have bold coloring,

just like a clown's painted face.

Crab

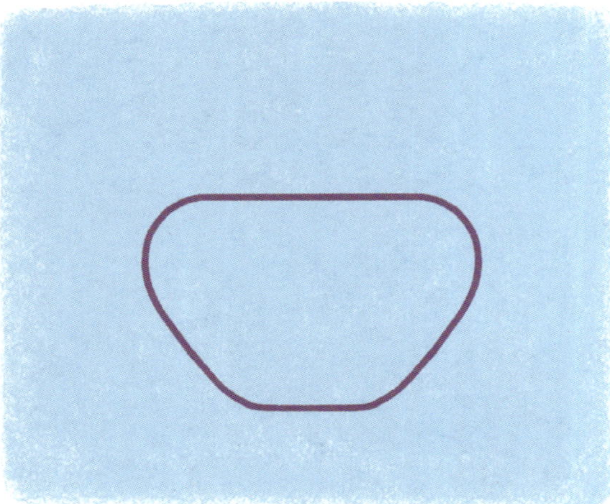

1 Begin with the body.

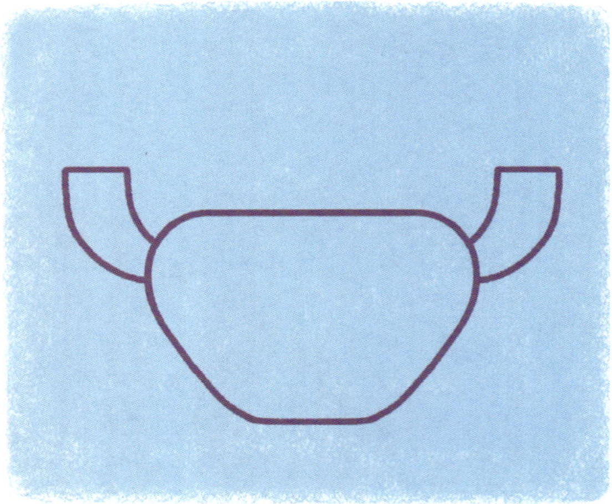

2 Add two front legs.

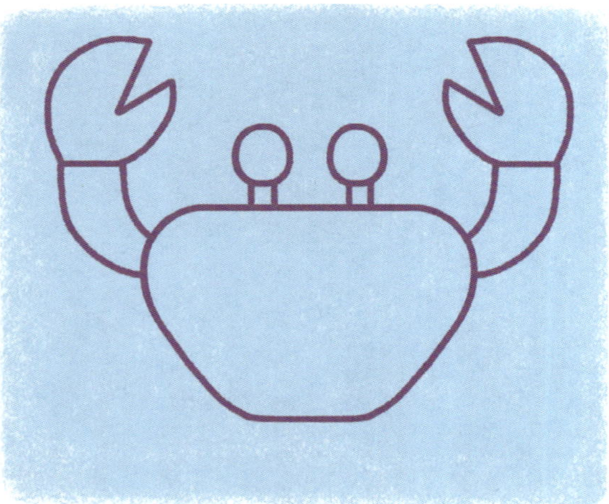

3 Draw two big claws and two eyes. They are on stalks so he can see all around.

4 Finish the face and add his six back legs. Color the crab bright orange.

Now try a hermit crab.

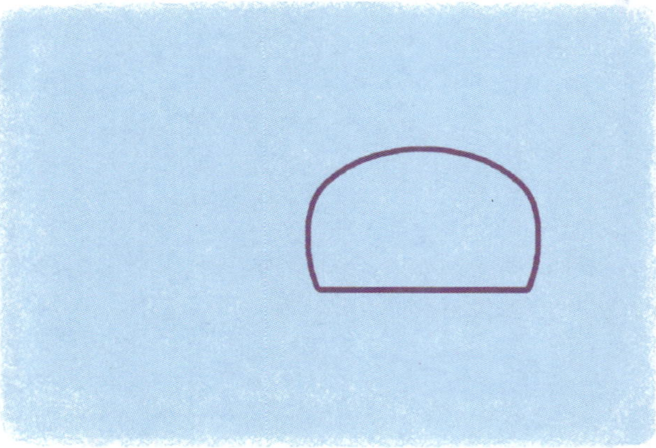

1 First, draw this shape for the body.

2 Next, add the little legs.

3 Add eyes, front legs, and claws.

4 Add the bumpy shell, and color an orange face.

Hermit crabs use old shells as their homes.

Stingray

1 Make a shape like this for the head and body.

2 Now draw a little fin at the end of the body.

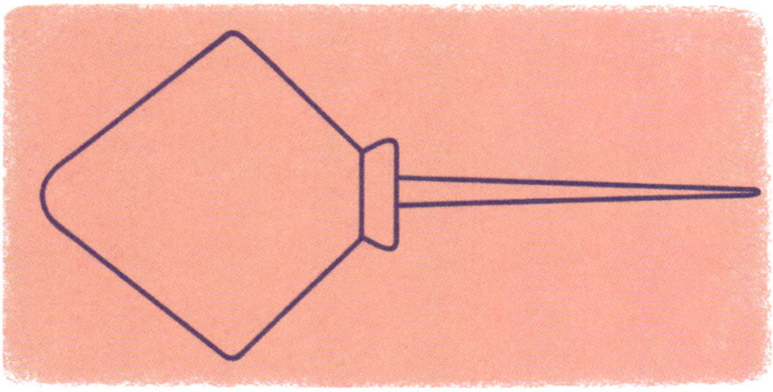

3 The tail is really long and pointed, like a sword.

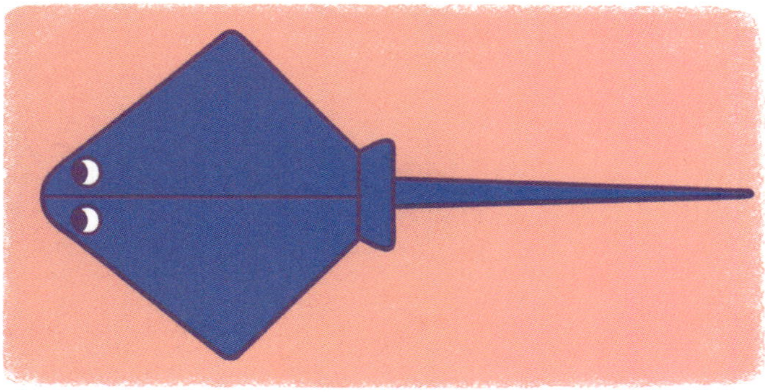

4 Add the eyes, then draw a line from the nose to the tail. Color the stingray bright blue.

Sea Snake

1 Start with half a circle for the head and a long neck.

2 Add two "U" shapes to make the curvy body.

3 Add one more before finishing with the tail.

4 Draw an eye and a forked tongue. Add some bold, black and white stripes.

Octopus

1 Begin with a rounded head.

2 Draw two outer arms.

3 The octopus needs six more arms!

4 Give it a happy face and make it a bright shade of orange.

Octopuses use their eight arms to seize fish and crabs to eat.

Dolphin

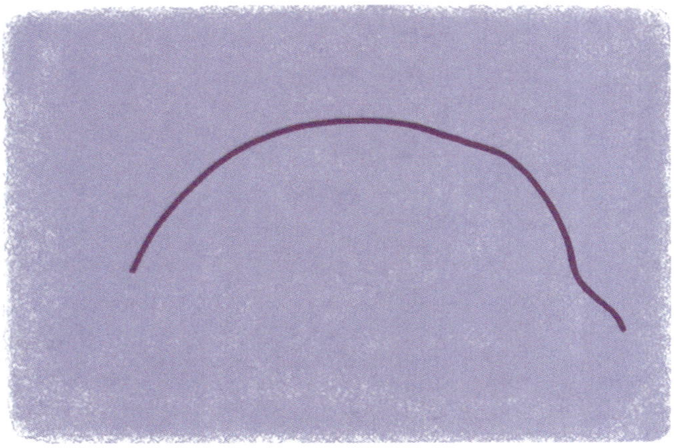

1 Start with a curved line for the dolphin's back.

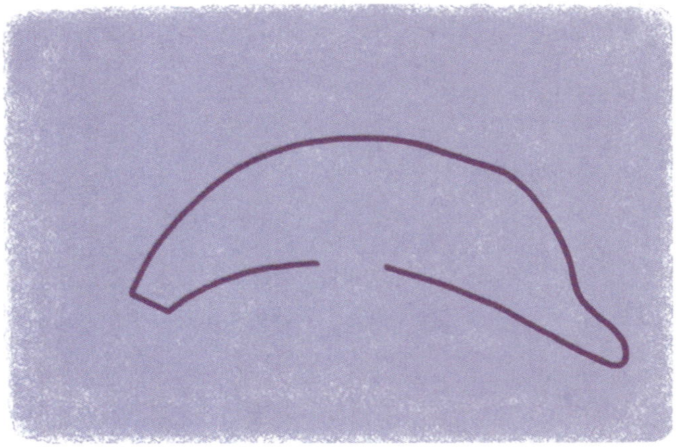

2 Now draw its tummy. Leave a gap for the flipper!

3 Add a fin on the back and two flippers.

4 Finish your drawing by adding an eye, mouth, and tail.

Jellyfish

1 First, draw this shape for the head.

2 Draw the bottom of the head with a wavy edge.

3 Add six long, wiggly lines.

4 Draw the face. Color it a pretty shade of pink.

Seahorse

1 Begin by drawing the head.

2 Then draw the body.

3 Add a cute, curly tail.

4 Add a fin and a crown. Add a face and lines on the tummy.

Make your seahorse any shade you like.

Seahorses aren't horses at all—they're fish!

Blue Whale

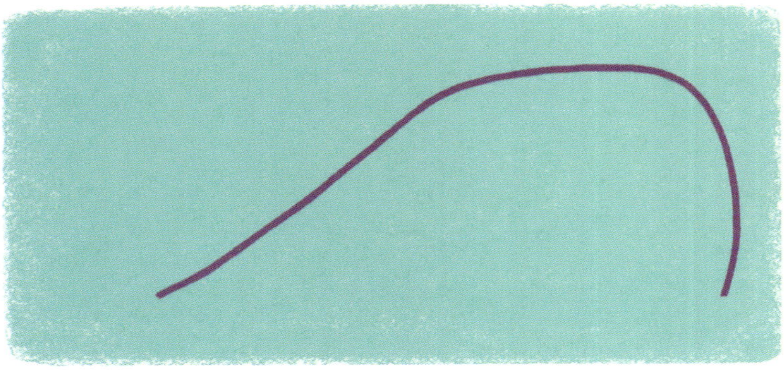

1 First, draw this shape for the top of the body.

2 Then draw a line for the tummy, and another line for a fin.

3 Add a big tail, and draw a line for the mouth.

4 Draw an eye, and add some lines under the mouth. Color it deep blue, like the sea.

Blue whales love to eat tiny krill!

Great White Shark

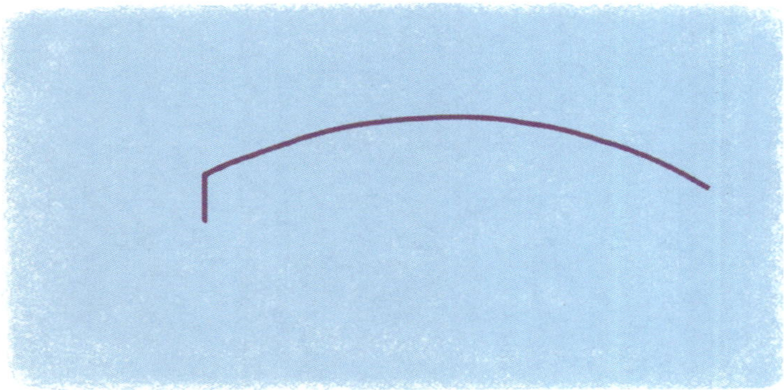

1 Start by drawing a curved line for the shark's back.

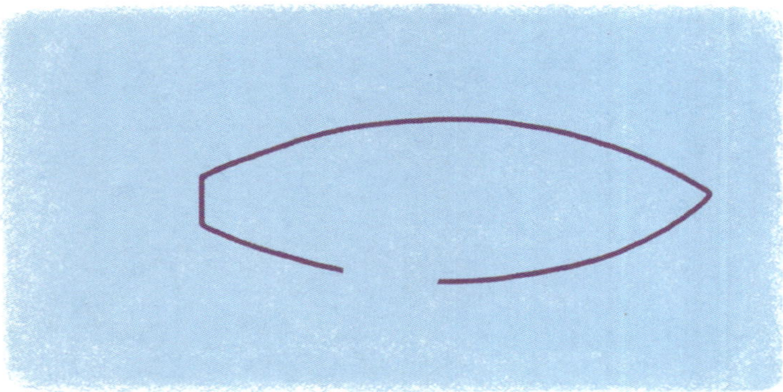

2 Now draw the tummy. Don't forget to leave a gap for the fin!

3 It needs a fin on the back and two fins underneath.

4 Finish by drawing an eye, a mouth, and a tail. The shark has very sharp teeth!

Now learn to draw a hammerhead shark.

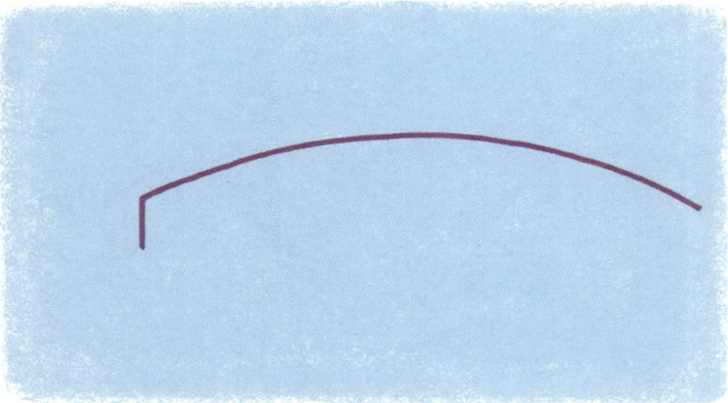

1 Begin in the same way, with a curved line for the back.

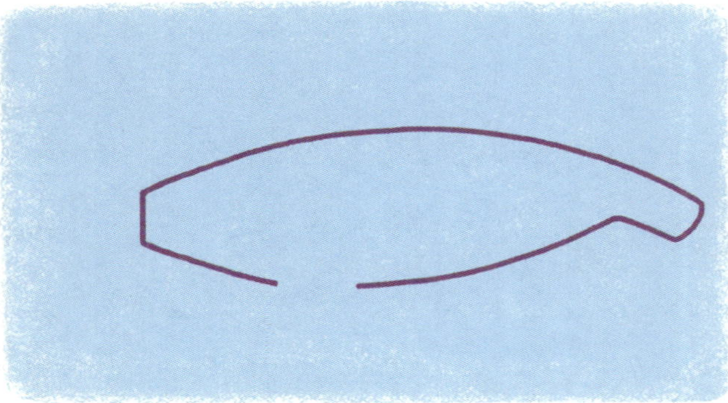

2 Now draw a tummy and one side of the head.

3 Add a fin on the back and two fins underneath.

4 Draw the other side of the head, two eyes, and a smiley mouth. What a friendly shark!

Turtle

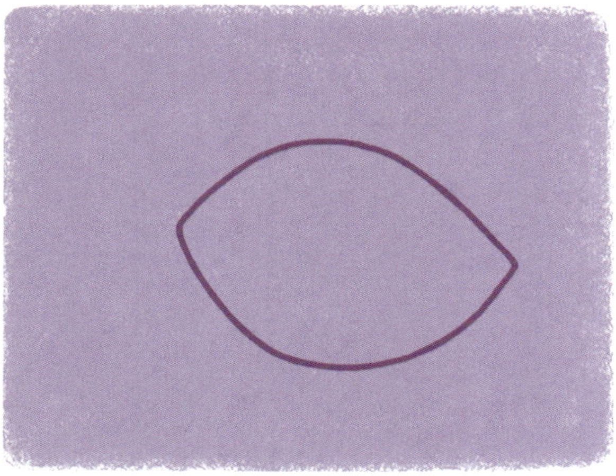

1 Begin by drawing this big shape for the shell.

2 Now add a little head at the front.

3 Draw four small flippers.

4 Draw a smiley face and a pattern on the shell. Color the turtle in different shades of green.

You can draw a tortoise in the same way!

It has a nice brown shell.

The tortoise has four short legs instead of flippers.

Tortoises usually live on land.

Turtles often live in the sea.

Glossary

claws The sharp nails on the feet of animals, birds, or sea creatures.

crown The top part of the head of an animal.

feelers The tentacles, or parts of a creature that help it to sense things around it.

fin A wing-like part of a fish that helps it to balance and swim.

flippers The wide, flat legs of sea creatures such as seals that are adapted for swimming.

forked Shaped like a fork, with one end divided into two or more branches.

hinge A joint on which something turns.

krill Tiny shellfish in the sea that are the main food of whales.

pearl A small, white jewel that grows inside some oysters.

pincer claws Claws that are used to grip objects.

seashore The beach, or land along the coast that gets wet when it is high tide and dry when the tide goes out.

tail fin The fin at the end of a fish or shellfish.

Further Information

Books

Clunes, Rebecca. *Drawing Sea Creatures*. New York, NY: Gareth Stevens Publishing, 2012.

Cuddy, Robbin. *Learn to Draw Sea Creatures*. Irvine, CA: Walter Foster Jr., 2014.

Farrell, Russell. *How to Draw Sea Creatures*. Lake Forest, CA: Walter Foster Jr., 2018.

Websites

www.artforkidshub.com/how-to-draw
This website uses videos to show you how to draw everything from seashells to sharks.

www.easypeasyandfun.com/how-to-draw
Learn how to draw an octopus, shark, whale, dolphin, and turtle, using video tutorials and printed templates.

Publisher's note to educators and parents: Our editors have carefully reviewed these websites to ensure that they are suitable for students. Many websites change frequently, however, and we cannot guarantee that a site's future contents will continue to meet our high standards of quality and educational value. Be advised that students should be closely supervised whenever they access the Internet.

Index